Q Pootle 5

EEEEEEEEEEEEEEE

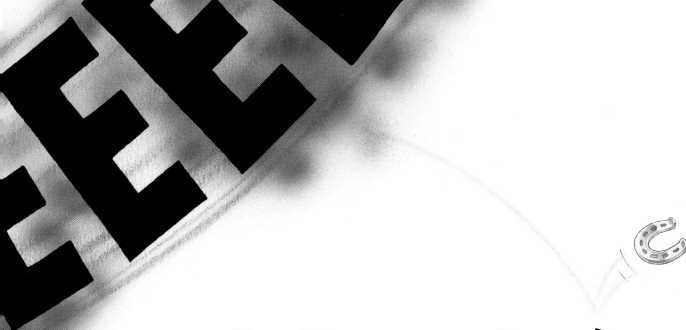

Q Pootle 5

NICK BUTTERWORTH

Collins

An imprint of HarperCollins*Publishers*

Q Pootle 5 has landed.

He has come to earth. But earth is not where Q Pootle 5 wants to be.

He is on his way to a moon party for his friend Z Pootle 6, but something has gone wrong.

Q Pootle 5 has a problem with his
spaceship. One of the rocket boosters
won't boost. The spaceship won't fly.
Q Pootle 5 looks carefully at the
rocket booster.

"Hmm," he says. He thinks he
knows what is wrong with it.
"It's just as I thought," he says.
"It's broken."

The spaceship needs a new rocket booster.

But where on earth can he find one?

Ah! Here comes an earthling. Perhaps he knows. He looks friendly and he is a nice colour. Green.

"Please can you help?" says Q Pootle 5.
"I need a rocket booster."

The earthling can't help. He doesn't even know what a rocket booster is.
Never mind. Here come some more earthlings. Perhaps they can help.

"Excuse me," says Q Pootle 5.
"Do you know where I can find
a new rocket booster?"
The earthlings think
very hard.

"No," says the first one. "Sorry."

"We don't use rocket boosters,"
says the second.

"We're birds," says the third earthling.

"Oh dear," says Q Pootle 5. "I'm going to
be late for the party."

But here comes another earthling.

And look! The earthling is carrying a
rocket booster!

What luck.

"Please," says Q Pootle 5,
"can you help me?"

He tells the earthling about his spaceship
and how it won't fly without a new
rocket booster.
"You can have this one,"
the earthling says.
"As soon as I
finish my dinner."

The earthling is called Colin.

He is pleased to help.

As soon as Colin has finished his dinner,
Q Pootle 5 fixes the new rocket booster
onto the spaceship.

Q Pootle 5 climbs into his spaceship.
He presses the starter button,
but nothing happens.
"Oh, beeebotherboootle!" says
Q Pootle 5. "I'm going to be late
and Z Pootle 6 will be upset."

Colin looks carefully at the spaceship.

"I'm not very clever with rockets," he says,

"but I think I can see the problem."

Colin knows why the spaceship won't fly.

"Can you pass me a spoon?" he says.

"There's a bit of my dinner stuck

in your rocket booster."

Now the rocket booster is clear.

Q Pootle 5 presses the starter button.

There is a rumbling sound, then a BANG!

followed by a funny smell that smells

a bit like Colin's dinner…

only cooked.

Q Pootle 5 pushes the starter button again. Hooray! The spaceship whooshes up into the air. Q Pootle 5 waves goodbye to Colin and the birds and the green earthling.
And they wave back.

Goodbye, Q Pootle 5.

Enjoy the moon party!

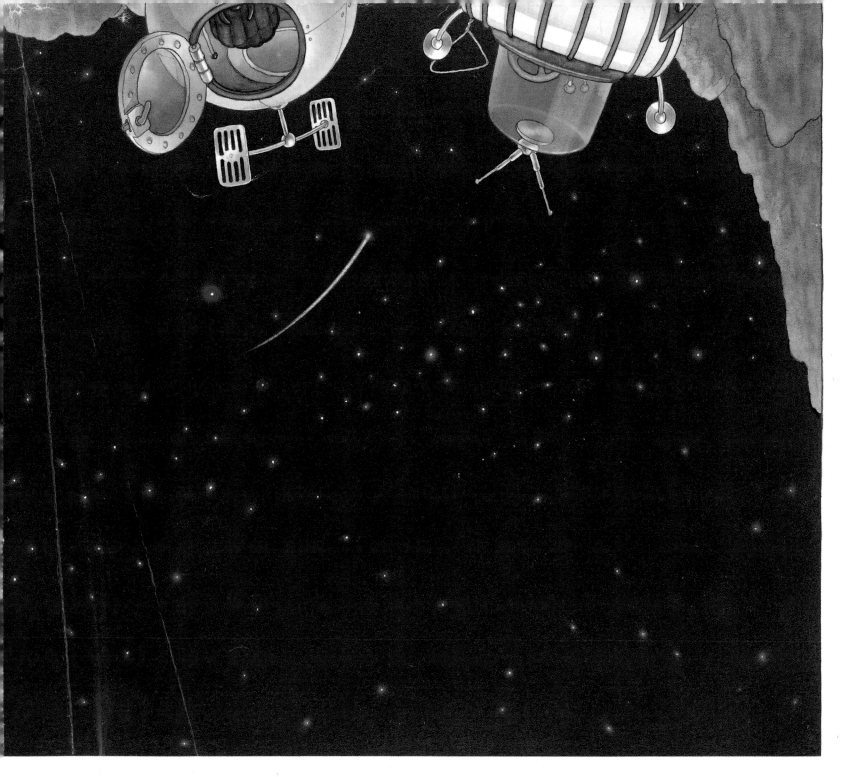

Then, suddenly…

just as suddenly as it came…

the spaceship is gone.

If you have enjoyed this book you'll love reading these other titles by Nick Butterworth.

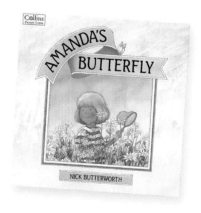

First published in hardback in Great Britain by HarperCollins Publishers Ltd in 2000
First published in paperback by Collins Picture Books in 2001
1 3 5 7 9 10 8 6 4 2
ISBN: 0-00-664712-X
Text and illustrations copyright © Nick Butterworth 2000
The author asserts the moral right to be identified as the author of the work.
A CIP catalogue record for this title is available from the British Library.
The HarperCollins website address is: www.**fire**and**water**.com
Manufactured in China